WRITTEN BY

Ann Dixon

ILLUSTRATED BY

Mark Graham

Merry Birthday,
Nora Noël

William B. Eerdmans Publishing Company

GRAND RAPIDS, MICHIGAN   CAMBRIDGE, U.K.

Copyright © 1996 Wm. B. Eerdmans Publishing Co.
Illustrations © 1996 Mark Graham
255 Jefferson Ave. S.E., Grand Rapids, Michigan 49503
P.O. Box 163, Cambridge   CB3   9PU   U.K.
All rights reserved

Printed in Hong Kong

00 99 98 97 96   7 6 5 4 3 2 1

Library of Congress Cataloging-in-Publication Data
Dixon, Ann.
Merry Birthday, Nora Noël / by Ann Dixon ; illustrated by Mark Graham.
p.   cm.
Summary: Nora Noël's father tells her the story of how the whole family looked forward
to her arrival and how they celebrated her birth as their own Christmas baby.
ISBN 0-8028-5105-3
[1. Babies — Fiction.   2. Birthdays — Fiction.   3. Christmas — Fiction.]
I. Graham, Mark, 1950 –   ill.   II Title.
PZ7.D642Me   1996
[E] — dc20   96-30392
*   CIP*
*   AC*

Designed by Joy Chu

To all Christmas babies, especially the First — A.D.

To Elizabeth and Bunzo — M.G.

*W*hen the earth

is frozen into stillness

and night creeps upon us

at midday

the first Advent candle is lit,

small flame flickering bravely

through December darkness.

With hope for

good things to come,

each year we await the

Christmas babe.

You, too, Nora Noël,
came to us at Christmas,
a baby as helpless and new
as any other.
But our waiting for you
lasted longer than Christmas,
longer than Advent,
longer, even, than winter.

This story is yours, Nora Noël.
Come sit on my lap, and
I will tell it to you
candle by candle,
season by season.

You began with the spring
as days grew longer,
earth waking into life.
Pussy willows bulged, soft as cat's paws.
"Is this spring?" asked James.
"I think so," said Anna.

While we waited and watched,
your mother napped
and didn't feel like eating.
"Mama's no fun," complained James.
"Why is she always tired?" asked Anna.
"Be patient," I told them. "Soon, I hope,
we will have good news."

*T*oday

when snowflakes

swarm to earth,

falling headlong

through dusk into darkness,

two Advent candles are lit,

partners in brightening the night.

With peace in our hearts

we look forward to the

Christmas babe.

As for you, Nora Noël,
you brightened
even the summer.
By then we knew
you really were coming.
Outside, in our garden,
the flowers grew.
Inside, so did you.
So did your mother!
Not in height,
but in rosy roundness.
She told us you fluttered
like a butterfly inside her,
speaking with gentle wings
the mysterious language of babes.
Your mother understood.
Peacefully she listened
to each message
you sent.

Now, when the sun

tucks us in for another

cold, long night with

a blanket of pink and

tangerine dreams,

three Advent candles are lit,

a cheerful crowd

upon the table.

With joy in the season

we prepare for the

Christmas babe.

But you, Nora Noël, brought dreams
we could hold and touch.
Blankets of many colors appeared—
gifts of soft flannel swaddling,
thick, downy quilts,
coverlets knit with joy and pleasure
to cozy our autumn dreams.

We felt and listened and watched
for each bumping, bulging motion.
"Can you hear us?" asked Anna.
"Don't kick Mama!" scolded James
until we laughed
and I explained how you were growing.

Today, when

the sun skims the rim

of a smooth blue sky

and night rises

full of moonlight,

four Advent candles are lit,

a promise we know

won't be broken.

With faith in the power

of light we welcome the

Christmas babe—

tomorrow!

And you, Nora Noël, kept your promise
spoken in months of flutter, kick, and dream.
On Christmas Eve, we were ready.
Presents waited under the tree for "Baby."
We took turns rocking your cradle,
just for practice.

The table was set, candles lit,
but Mama was restless,
too restless for food.
While we opened packages,
she paced.
"Soon," she assured us,
"our baby will be here."

*N*ow, as night
overtakes the sun,
our brief reminder,
and the moon shines
clear and cold,
five candles are lit,
their blaze reflected in
the stars, our hearts.
With light and love
we give thanks for the
Christmas babe.

Nora Noël, you greeted us
with a cry of surprise
at a world so vast
and unknown.
Mama held you close, heart to heart,
until you understood that love is here.
I murmured my welcomes
and stroked your cheek.
You gave a sigh that fluttered through us.
Your eyes opened, wide and
 deep as the heavens.
"You're so soft!" whispered Anna,
holding fingers tightly curled.
"You're so little!" said James, standing tall.
"You're Nora Noël," Mama told you.
We all agreed
and gave thanks for our own
Christmas babe.

A Note about Advent

Advent is a season of preparation celebrated by Christians around the world. The word Advent comes from a Latin verb meaning "to come." For most Christians, Advent begins four Sundays prior to Christmas and culminates on Christmas Day. In the Greek and Russian churches, Advent begins six weeks before Christmas.

In this story, the tradition of the Advent wreath, which originated in Germany and Scandinavia, is honored. One candle is lit each Sunday, with the fifth lit on Christmas Day. In the order of lighting, the candles represent hope, peace, joy, faith, and finally, love.

Although Advent traditions vary, the reason for observing Advent remains the same: to prepare our hearts for welcoming God's gift of light and love, his son Jesus.